BRAIN GAMES™ kids

PRESCHOOL

Illustrations by Michele Ackerman, Marie Allen, Martha Avilés, Tiphanie Beeke, Michelle Berg, Louise Gardner, Kallen Godsey, Thea Kliros, Kate Kolososki, Jane Maday, Michael Miller, Margie Moore, Robin Moro, Nicholas Myers, Ryan Sias, Peggy Tagel, George Ulrich, Ted Williams, David Wojtowycz, and Maria Woods

Photography by Art Explosion, Dreamstime, ImageClub, Jupiter Images Unlimited, PhotoDisc, Siede Preis Photography, Shutterstock, and Brian Warling Photography

Customer Service: 1-800-595-8484 or customer_service@pilbooks.com

www.pilbooks.com

p i kids is a registered trademark of Publications International, Ltd.
Brain Games is a trademark of Publications International, Ltd.

8 7 6 5 4 3 2 1

Manufactured in China.

ISBN-10: 1-4508-0052-1
ISBN-13: 978-1-4508-0052-5

publications international, ltd.

Letter to Parents

Welcome to Brain Games!

Get ready for an exciting kind of early-learning activity! These 301 questions tackle key benchmarks across core categories such as language arts and math, as well as science, social sciences, physical and emotional development, fine arts, and foreign language. Each left-hand page contains one to four questions; each right-hand page supplies concrete answers. Categories are scattered throughout the book, and questions progress from easy to hard for a graduated learning experience. Colorful illustrations and photography help to present the material in a fun and engaging way. Settle down, open the book, and have fun learning with your child today!

How to Use

- Open to the desired set of questions and answers. Fold the book in half so you and your child see only the questions.

- Read the questions aloud. Ask your child to point to or name the answer.

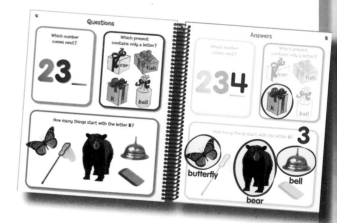

- Flip the book over to reveal the answers. The answers are shown in red. Miss a few? Don't worry! Every child develops a little differently—go back and try these questions again in a few days or even months. Build confidence and continue at a pace that is comfortable for your child.

Which cat is smaller?

Which building is the tallest?

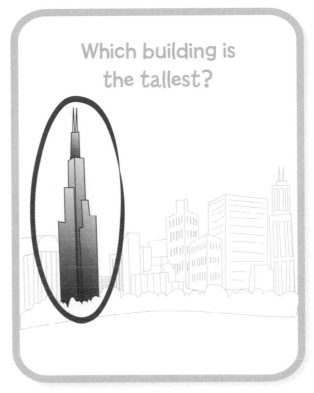

Which of these is a musical instrument?

drum

Which animal is feeling sick?

Questions

Which snake is longer?

Are there more purple or green crayons?

How many fingers are held up in this picture?

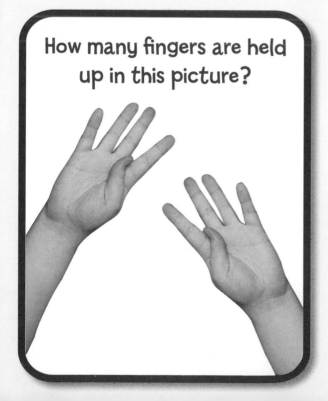

Which of these objects begins with the letter K?

Which snake is longer?

Are there more purple or green crayons?

purple

How many fingers are held up in this picture?

1 2 3
4
6 7 8
5

8

Which of these objects begins with the letter K?

kite

Questions

Which number comes next?

45_

Which letter comes next?

Which letter comes next?

Which two pictures rhyme?

Which number comes next?

4 5 6

Which letter comes next?

I J **K**

Which letter comes next?

C D **E**

Which two pictures rhyme?

hat

cat

Do you see the letter **C** hidden 7 times in this picture?

Can you name each of the 7 objects?

How many blue things do you see?

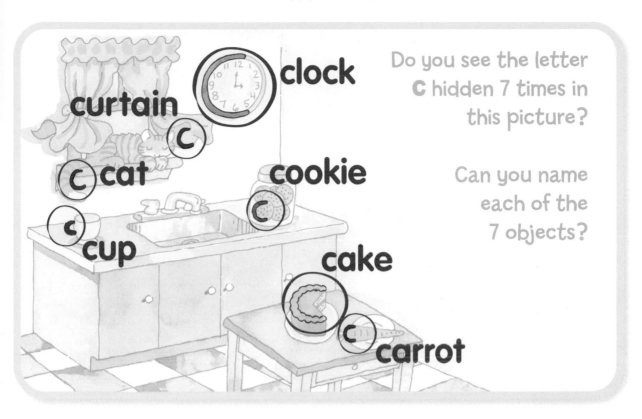

clock

curtain

c

cat

c

cup

cookie

c

cake

carrot

Do you see the letter **c** hidden 7 times in this picture?

Can you name each of the 7 objects?

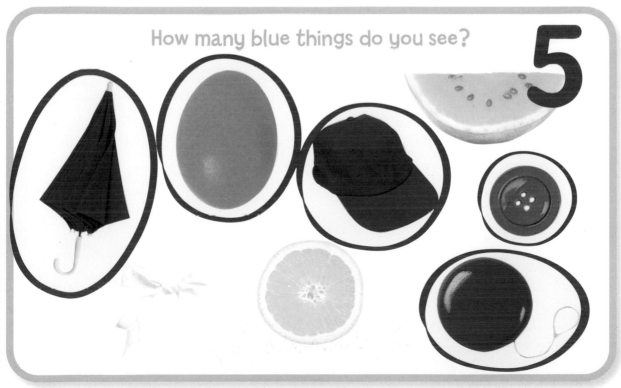

How many blue things do you see?

5

Questions

Which letter comes next?

Which two pictures rhyme?

How many yellow things do you see?

Which letter comes next?

F G **H**

Which two pictures rhyme?

box

fox

How many yellow things do you see?

5

Questions

Which of these objects begin with the letter C?

Is the bunny happy or angry?

How many black things do you see?

Answers

Which of these objects begin with the letter **C**?

Is the bunny happy or **angry**?

How many black things do you see?

6

Questions

Which toy costs more?

$3

$7

Which plate is full?

Which one means "good-bye" in Spanish?

hola

adiós

Which two pictures rhyme?

Which toy costs more?

$3

$7

Which plate is full?

Which one means "good-bye" in Spanish?

hola

adiós

Which two pictures rhyme?

bee

tree

Questions

What is this picture?
What is its first letter?

_at

What is the
cat wearing?

How many fingers are held
up in this picture?

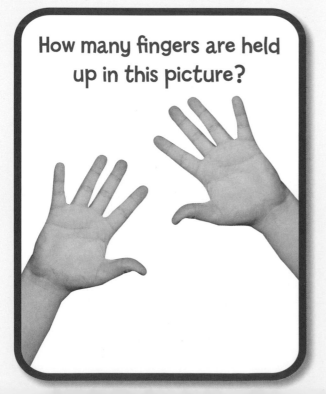

What is this picture?
What is its first letter?

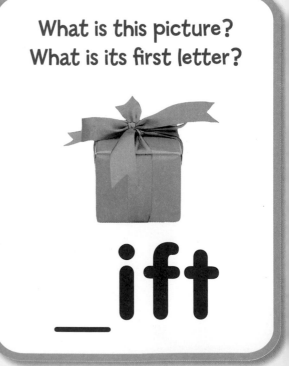

_ift

What is this picture?
What is its first letter?

bat

What is the
cat wearing?

hat

How many fingers are held
up in this picture?

8 9 10

7

1 2 3

4

6

5

10

What is this picture?
What is its first letter?

gift

Which letter comes next?

HI _

Is the puppy inside or outside the house?

What is this picture?
What is its first letter?

_ree

What shape is the tent?

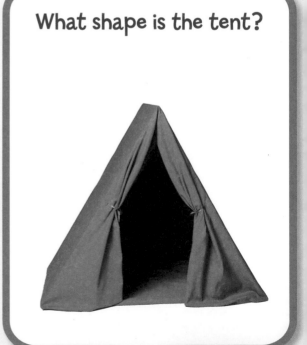

Which letter comes next?

H I J

Is the puppy **inside** or outside the house?

What is this picture?
What is its first letter?

tree

What shape is the tent?

triangle

Questions

Do you see the letter D hidden in the picture?

Which animal is slower?

How many orange things do you see?

Do you see the letter **D** hidden in the picture?

Which animal is slower?

turtle

How many orange things do you see?

6

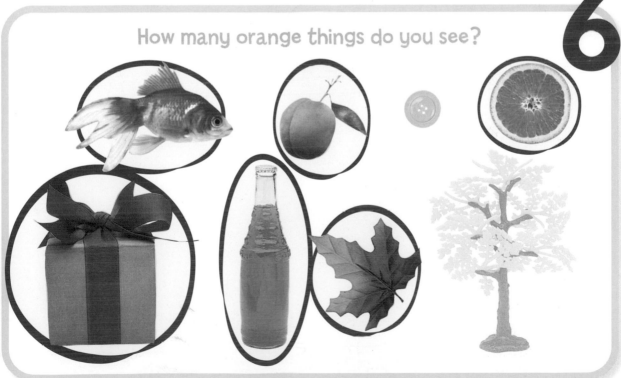

Question

How many things in this picture start with the letter **T**?

How many things in this picture start with the letter **T**?

turtle

5

tree

teacher

table

truck

Questions

What season is it in this picture?

Do you see the letter Z hidden in the bowl of soup?

Which one of these is not an insect?

Which food starts with the letter P?

Answers

What season is it in this picture?

winter

Do you see the letter **Z** hidden in the bowl of soup?

Which one of these is not an insect?

flamingo

Which food starts with the letter **P**?

pear

Questions

How many things start with the letter H?

How many koalas do you see?

How many things start with the letter C?

How many things start with the letter H?

3

hammer **heart**   **hot dog**

How many koalas do you see?

3

How many things start with the letter C?

2

castle   **carrot**

Questions

How many green things do you see?

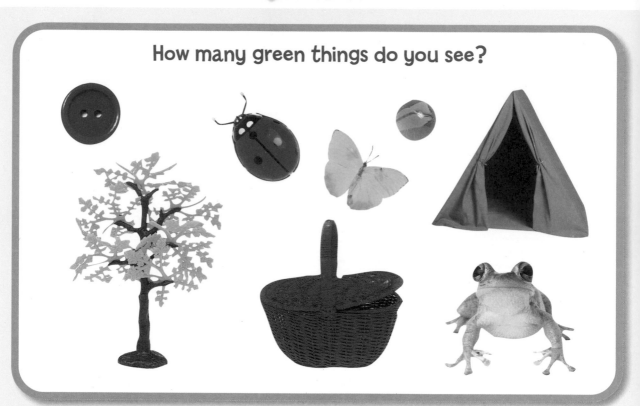

Are there more gorillas or goats?

4

How many green things do you see?

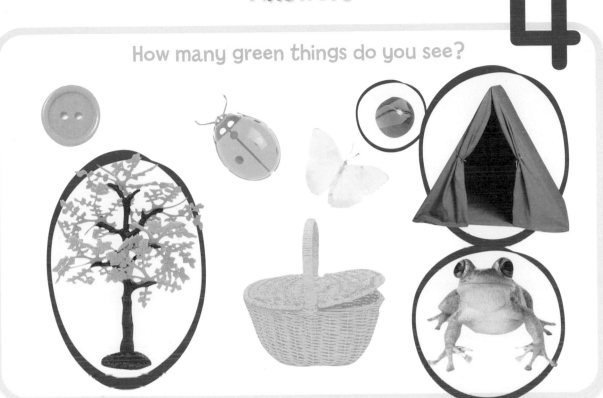

Are there more gorillas or goats?

Questions

What is the bear holding?

What is this picture? What is its first letter?

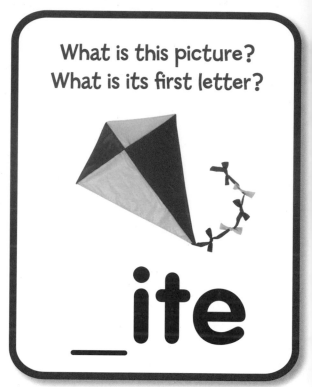

_ite

How many brown things do you see?

What is the
bear holding?

pear

What is this picture?
What is its first letter?

<u>k</u>ite

How many brown things do you see?

7

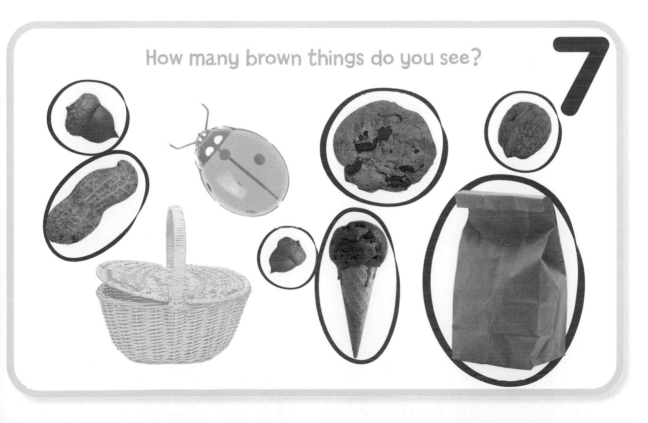

Questions

Which number comes next?

56_____

Which one means "please" in Spanish?

el cerdo

por favor

Which two pictures rhyme?

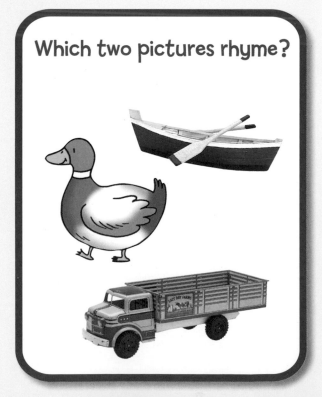

Which box is closed?

Which number comes next?

567

Which one means "please" in Spanish?

el cerdo

por favor

Which two pictures rhyme?

duck

truck

Which box is closed?

Questions

How many rockets do you see?

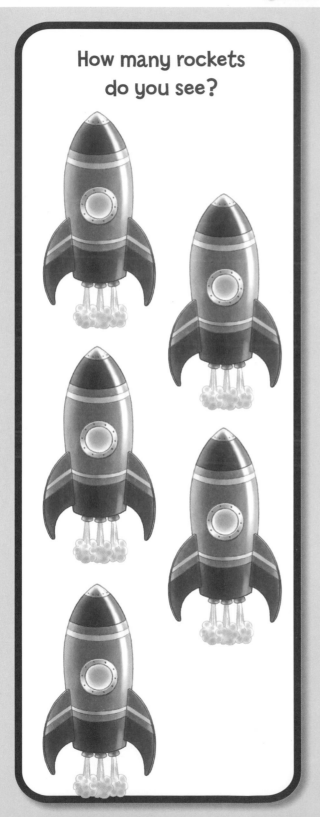

What is the correct order for these pictures?

How many rockets
do you see?

5

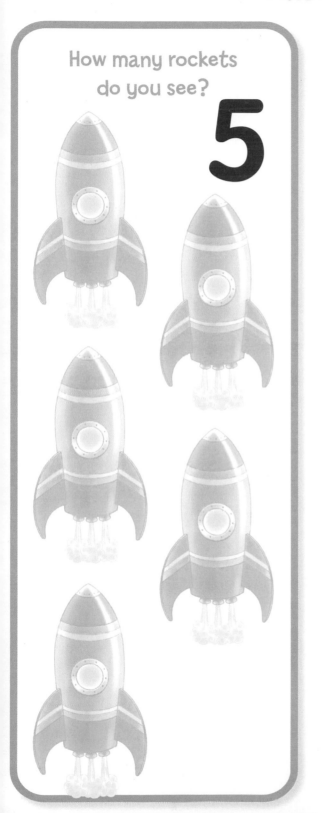

What is the correct order
for these pictures?

Questions

Which food starts with the letter I?

What is this picture? What is its first letter?

_ee

What shape is the badge?

Which two pictures rhyme?

Which food starts with the letter I?

ice cream

What is this picture? What is its first letter?

bee

What shape is the badge?

star

Which objects rhyme?

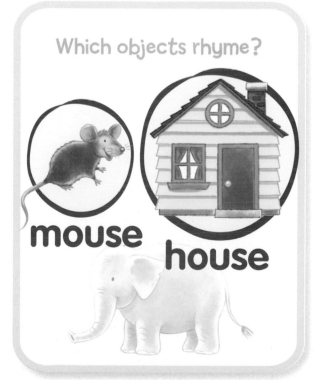

mouse

house

Question

How many umbrellas can you find in this picture?

How many umbrellas can you find in this picture?

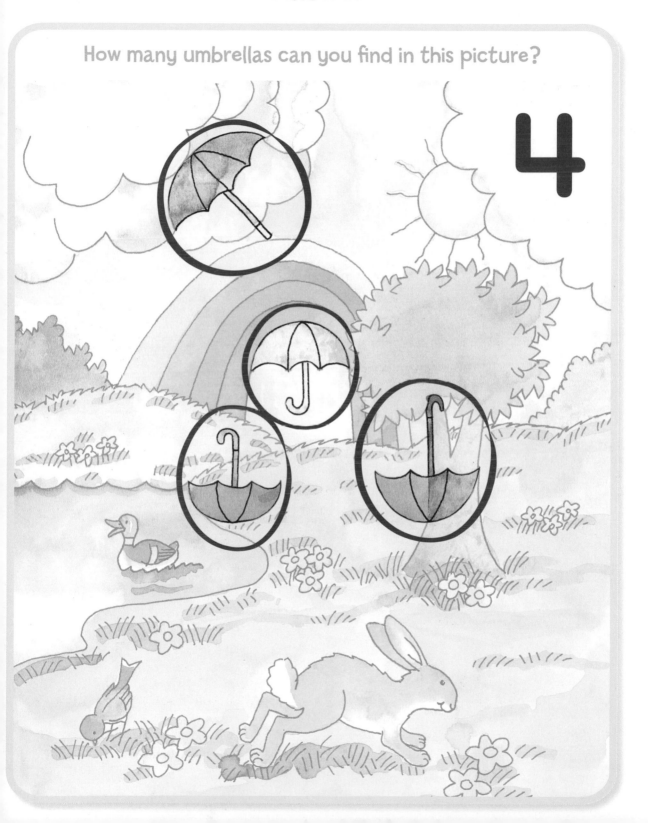

Questions

Which animal purrs when it is happy?

Which bunny is in the hat?

Which car faces front?

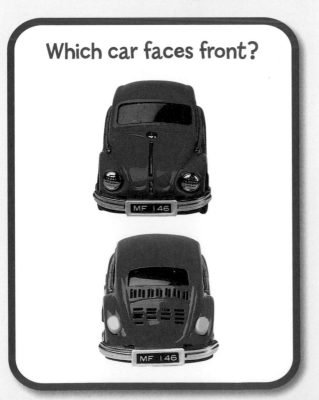

Which plant is the youngest?

Which animal purrs when it is happy?

cat

Which bunny is in the hat?

Which car faces front?

Which plant is the youngest?

Questions

How many things start with the letter **G**?

Are there more zebras or buses?

How many things start with the letter **S**?

2

How many things start with the letter **G**?

glasses **grapes**

Are there more zebras or **buses**?

3

How many things start with the letter **S**?

starfish **spider** **spoon**

Questions

Do you see the letter **I** hidden 4 times in this picture?

How many red things do you see?

Do you see the letter **I** hidden 4 times in this picture?

How many red things do you see?

7

Questions

Do you see the letter **T** hidden in the picture?

Which picture matches the word?

boat

Which animal is the opposite of small?

Which of these objects begins with the letter **A**?

Do you see the letter **T** hidden in the picture?

Which picture matches the word?

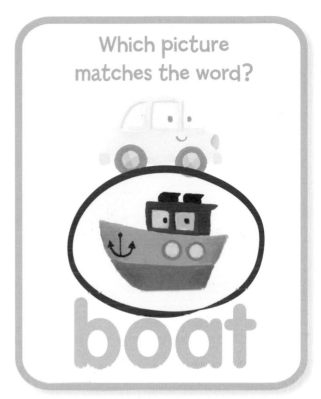

boat

Which animal is the opposite of small?

big

Which of these objects begins with the letter **A**?

apple

Questions

Which dog is the opposite of wet?

How many fingers are held up in this picture?

Are there more pumpkins or oranges?

Which dog is the opposite of wet?

dry

How many fingers are held up in this picture?

3 1 2 3

Are there more pumpkins or (oranges)?

Questions

Which gift is on the left?

Which paint can is open?

Which number comes next?

78_

Which letter comes next?

Which gift is on the left?

Which paint can is open?

Which number comes next?

7 8 **9**

Which letter comes next?

Questions

Which two pictures rhyme?

Which bee is under the flower?

How many objects start with the letter **P**?

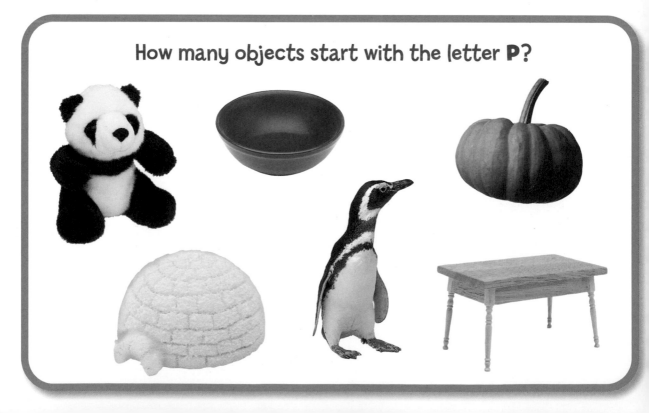

Answers

Which two pictures rhyme?

snake

cake

Which bee is under the flower?

How many objects start with the letter **P**?

3

panda

penguin

pumpkin

Questions

How many apples are in the tree?

Which plate has more cookies?

Do you see the letter **B** hidden in this picture 3 times?

How many apples are in the tree?

5

Which plate has more cookies?

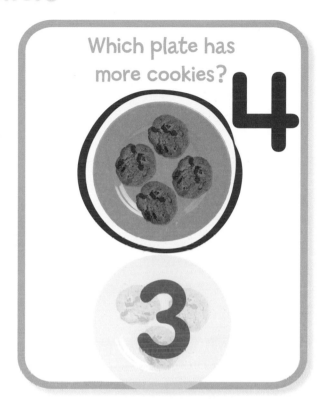

4

3

Do you see the letter **B** hidden in this picture 3 times?

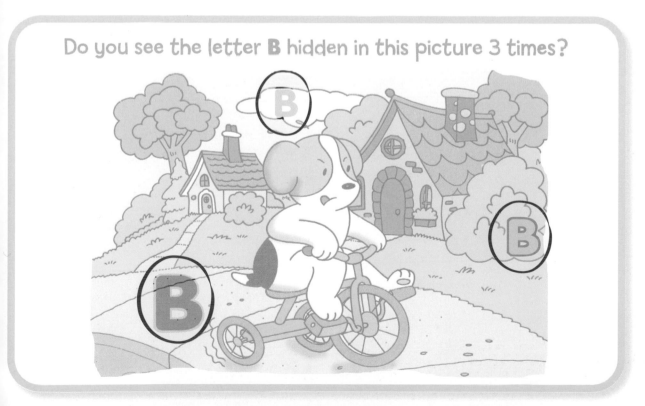

Questions

How many trucks are there?

Do you see the letter **P** hidden in this picture 4 times?

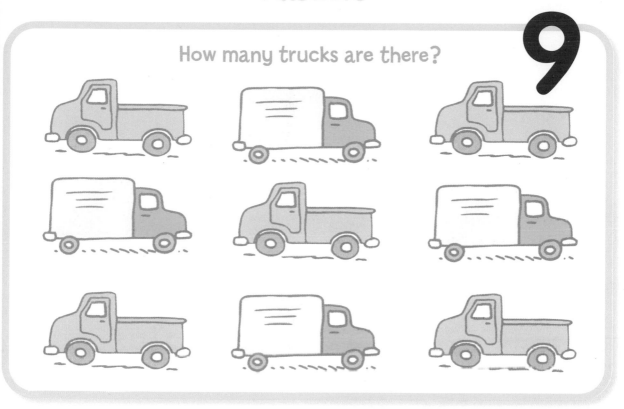

Answers

How many trucks are there?

9

Do you see the letter **P** hidden in this picture 4 times?

Questions

How many bells are there?

Which letter comes next?

Do you see the letter **G** hidden in this picture 2 times?

What is the correct first letter for this word?

_tar

How many bells are there?

5

Which letter comes next?

O P Q

Do you see the letter G hidden in this picture 2 times?

What is the correct first letter for this word?

star

Questions

Which of these objects begin with the letter **L**?

What shape is the yo-yo?

Which picture matches the word?

hat

How many buttons can you find on the bear?

Which of these objects begin with the letter L?

leaf

lion

What shape is the yo-yo?

circle

Which picture matches the word?

hat

How many buttons can you find on the bear?

3

Questions

Which letter comes next?

How many fingers are held up in this picture?

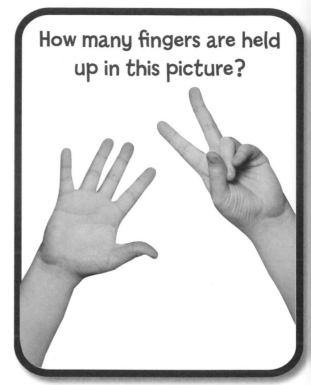

How many watermelon slices do you see?

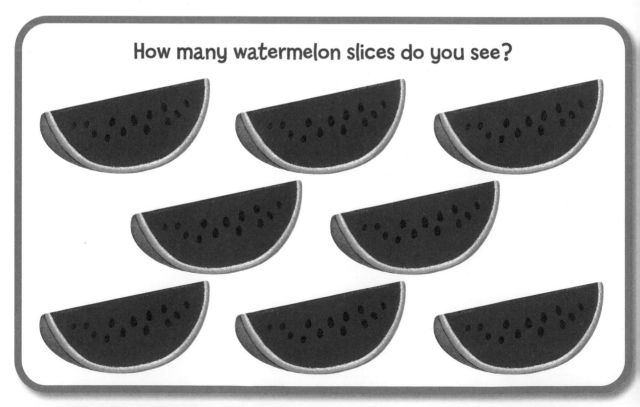

Which letter comes next?

How many fingers are held up in this picture?

How many watermelon slices do you see?

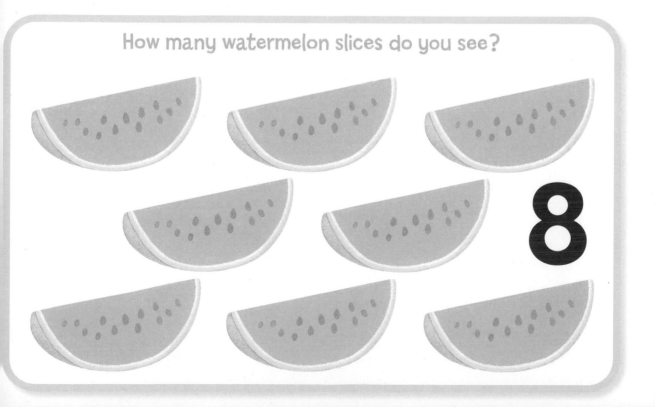

Questions

How many frogs
are there?

Which of these objects
begins with the letter **E**?

Which person
keeps you and your
neighborhood safe?

Which of these goes on
your feet?

How many frogs
are there?

4

Which of these objects
begins with the letter **E**?

elephant

Which person
keeps you and your
neighborhood safe?

police officer

Which of these goes on
your feet?

socks

Questions

How many birds
are there?

How many things start
with the letter **V**?

How many birds
are there? **3**

How many things start
with the letter **V**? **3**

violin

vase

van

Questions

How many fingers does this person have?

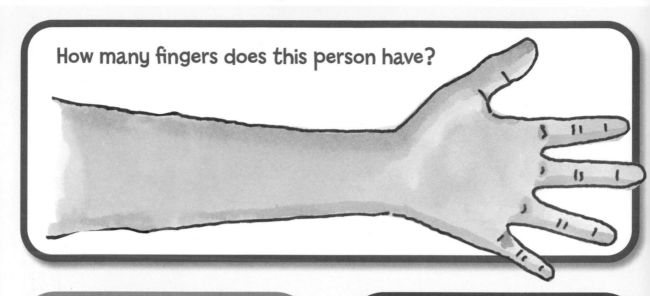

Which picture matches the word?

walrus

What shape is the door?

How many fingers does this person have?

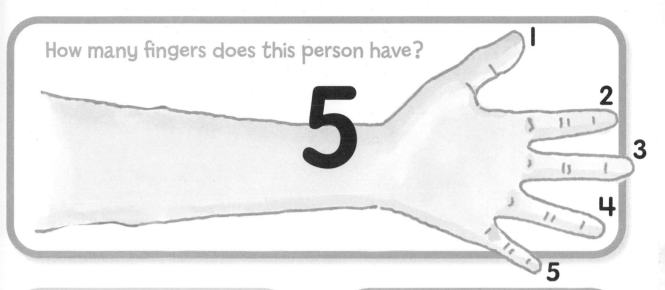

1
2
3
4
5

5

Which picture matches the word?

walrus

What shape is the door?

rectangle

Questions

Which two objects rhyme?

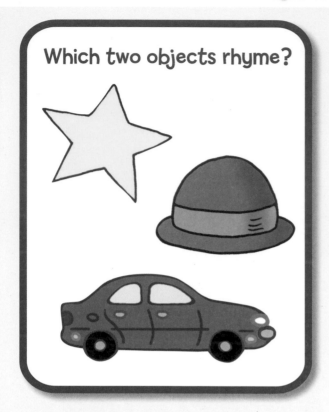

Which person is wearing glasses?

Which of these objects begin with the letter **o**?

Which letter comes next?

Answers

Which two objects rhyme?

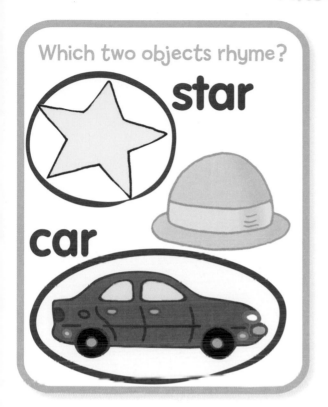

star

car

Which person is wearing glasses?

Which of these objects begin with the letter O?

owl

octopus

Which letter comes next?

Questions

Do you see the letter **K** hidden in this picture 4 times?

Which animal says moo?

How many petals are on the flower?

Which of these objects begin with the letter **S**?

Do you see the letter **K** hidden in this picture 4 times?

Which animal says moo? **COW**

How many petals are on the flower?

8

Which of these objects begin with the letter S? **shoe** **snake**

Questions

How many squirrels do you see?

How many animals have four legs?

Do you see the letter **H** hidden in this picture 5 times?

Answers

How many squirrels do you see?

6

How many animals have four legs?

3

Do you see the letter **H** hidden in this picture 5 times?

Questions

Do you see the letter **R** hidden in this picture 3 times?

What two shapes are in the ice-cream cone?

How many birds are in the tree?

Which two objects rhyme?

Answers

Do you see the letter **R** hidden in this picture 3 times?

What two shapes are in the ice-cream cone?

circle

triangle

How many birds are in the tree?

Which two objects rhyme?

plane

train

Questions

Which of these starts with the letter **W**?

How many fingers are held up in this picture?

Which plane is above the cloud?

Is the cat crying or smiling?

Which of these starts with the letter **W**?

whale

How many fingers are held up in this picture?

2

Which plane is above the cloud?

Is the cat crying or smiling?

Questions

Which side of the scale holds the heavier fruit?

Which of these objects begin with the letter **T**?

Which two animals rhyme?

How many tops are there?

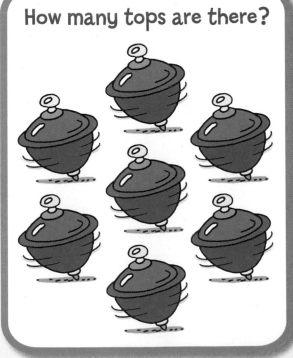

Which side of the scale holds the heavier fruit?

right

Which of these objects begin with the letter T?

turtle

train

Which two animals rhyme?

dog

frog

How many tops are there?

7

Questions

Which helper prepares food?

How many tigers are there?

Do you see the letter Z hidden in the picture 7 times?

Which helper prepares food?

chef

How many tigers are there?

3

Do you see the letter **Z** hidden in the picture 7 times?

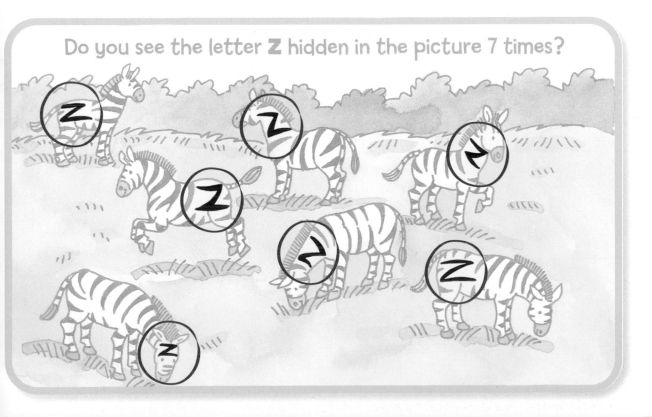

Questions

How many helicopters are there?

Which one is made from wool?

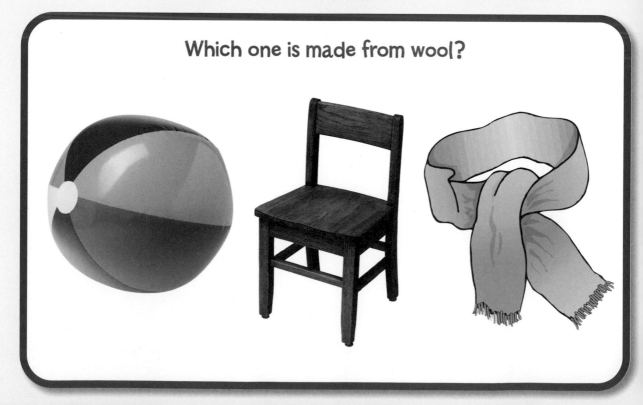

10

How many helicopters are there?

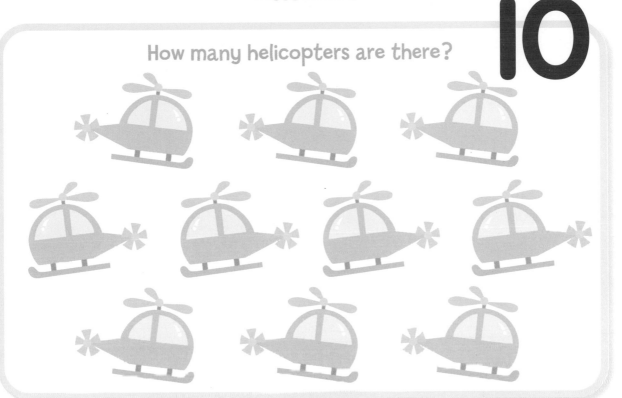

Which one is made from wool?

scarf

Questions

Which one is the dog?

Which two objects rhyme?

Which picture matches the word?

jar

Which one will stick to the magnet?

Answers

Which one is the dog?

Which two objects rhyme?

shake

cake

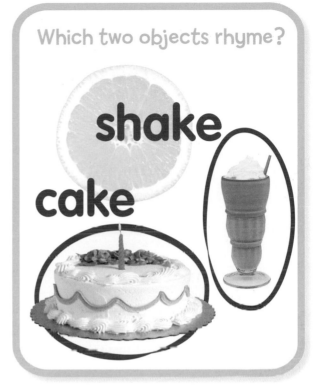

Which picture matches the word?

jar

Which one will stick to the magnet?

key

Questions

How many objects start with the letter J?

What is the correct order for these pictures?

How many objects start with the letter J?

2

jacket

jeans

What is the correct order for these pictures?

2

1

3

Questions

Which person has blue eyes?

How many quails do you see?

Which person helps you find books?

Which two objects rhyme?

Answers

Which person has blue eyes?

How many quails do you see? **6**

Which person helps you find books?

librarian

Which two objects rhyme?

clock
sock

Questions

Do you see the letter **F** hidden in the picture 6 times?

Look at the candles. How old is Puppy?

How many circles can you find in this scene?

Which picture matches the word?

star

Do you see the letter **F** hidden in the picture 6 times?

Look at the candles. How old is Puppy?

3

How many circles can you find in this scene?

8

Which picture matches the word?

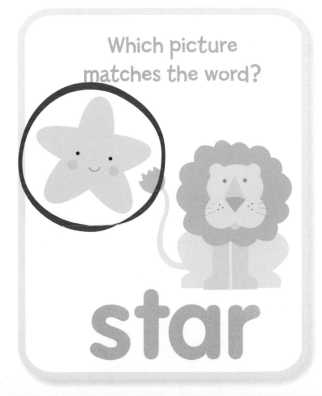

star

Question

Find all the things that start with the letter **y**.

Find all the things that start with the letter **y**.

yarn

yo-yo

YOGURT

CHERRY
WITH OTHER NATURAL FLAVORS

yogurt

Questions

Do you see the letter **S** hidden in the picture 5 times?

Which animal lives in the nest?

How many animals have spots?

Do you see the letter **S** hidden in the picture 5 times?

Which animal lives in the nest?

bird

How many animals have spots?

2

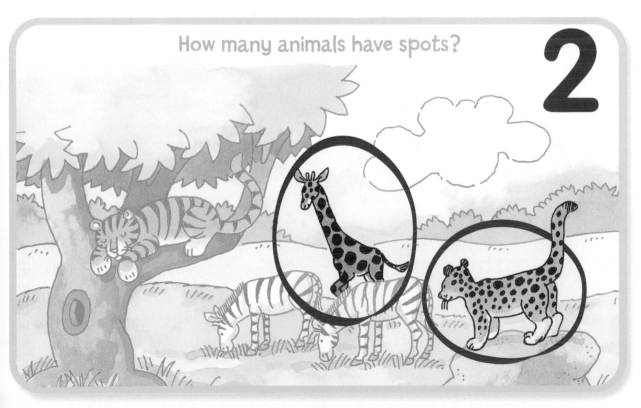

Questions

Do you see the letter **W** hidden in the picture 4 times?

Which child is not following the rules?

Which animal is exactly the same as the one in the circle?

Answers

Do you see the letter **W** hidden in the picture 4 times?

Which child is not following the rules?

He did not stop.

Which animal is exactly the same as the one in the circle?

Questions

How many rectangles do you see in the house?

Which ball is the same as the one in the square?

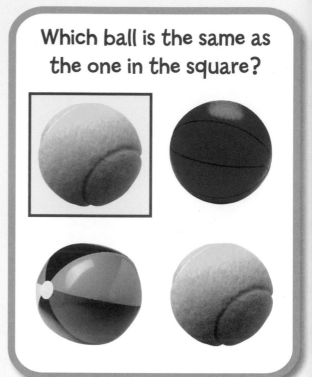

Which picture matches the word?

sun

What color button comes next?

How many rectangles do you see in the house?

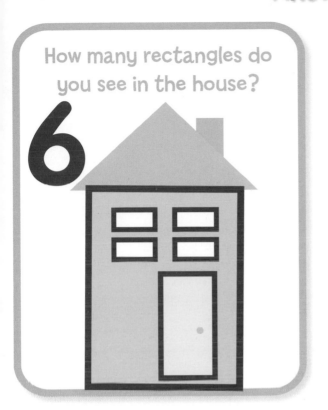

6

Which ball is the same as the one in the square?

Which picture matches the word?

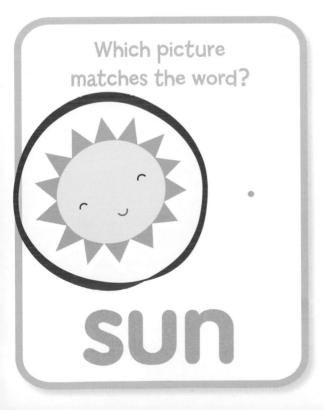

sun

What color button comes next?

blue

Questions

Which sea creature's name starts the same way as "jack"?

Which picture matches the word?

truck

Which creature made this web?

Which sea creature's name starts the same way as "jack"?

jellyfish

Which picture matches the word?

truck

Which creature made this web?

spider

Which picture
matches the word?

horse

Point to the Earth.

Which of these
is different?

How many monkeys are
jumping on the bed?

Answers

Which picture matches the word?

horse

Point to the Earth.

Which of these is different?

How many monkeys are jumping on the bed?

4

Questions

What color gift comes next?

Uh-oh! Hippo knocked the plant over. What should he say?

Thank you.
_____
I'm sorry.

Which of these starts the same way as "bat"?

What color gift comes next?

yellow

Uh-oh! Hippo knocked the plant over. What should he say?

Thank you.

I'm sorry.

Which of these starts the same way as "bat"?

butterfly

What is the correct first letter for this word?

_ish

How many red wagons are there?

Which picture matches the word?

lamb

Which animal can live in cold places?

What is the correct first letter for this word?

fish

How many red wagons are there?

3

Which picture matches the word?

lamb

Which animal can live in cold places?

penguin

Questions

Which food should the rabbit eat?

What is the correct first letter for this word?

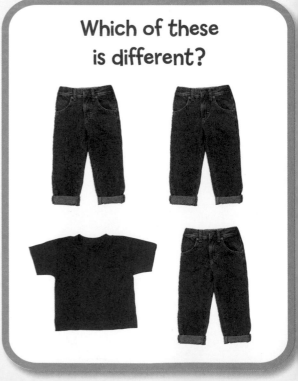

_og

Which one would you most likely see at Thanksgiving?

Which of these is different?

Which food should the rabbit eat?

carrot

What is the correct first letter for this word?

dog

Which one would you most likely see at Thanksgiving?

turkey

Which of these is different?

Which picture matches the word?

dinosaur

How many green trucks are there?

Which one would a baker wear?

What is the correct first letter for this word?

_ig

Which picture matches the word?

dinosaur

How many green trucks are there?

5

Which one would a baker wear?

What is the correct first letter for this word?

pig

Questions

Which one means "friend" in Spanish?

amigo

el gato

Which word starts the same way as "door"?

Find the things that start with the letter **R**.

Which one means "friend" in Spanish?

amigo

el gato

Which word starts the same way as "door"?

duck

Find the things that start with the letter **R**.

ring

rocket

Questions

Which picture starts the same way as "sun"?

Point to the American flag.

Which of these goes with the brush in the circle?

Which picture starts the same way as "sun"?

sailboat

Point to the American flag.

Which of these goes with the brush in the circle?

TOOTHPASTE

100%

KETCHUP

Questions

Which picture starts the same way as "egg"?

What do you brush before you go to bed?

Do you see the letter X hidden in the picture 5 times?

Which one means "stop"?

Which picture starts the same way as "egg"?

eraser

What do you brush before you go to bed?

teeth

Do you see the letter X hidden in the picture 5 times?

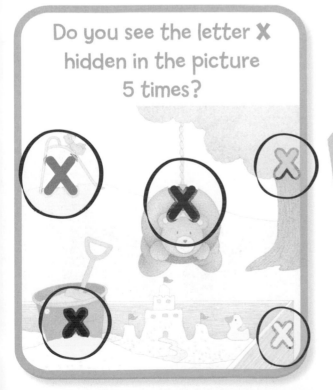

Which one means "stop"?

Questions

Which word starts the same way as "rock"?

Find all the things that start with the letter **W**.

Which word starts the
same way as "rock"?

robot

Find all the things that
start with the letter W

wolf

wheelchair

waffle

witch

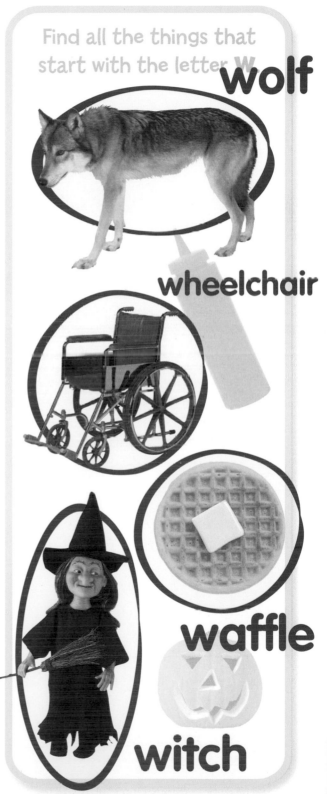

Question

How many yellow dogs are there?

6

How many yellow dogs are there?

Questions

Is the hat on or off the dog's head?

In this line, who is the closest to the teacher?

What's wrong with this picture?

139

Answers

Is the hat **on** or off the dog's head?

In this line, who is the closest to the teacher?

What's wrong with this picture?

Which drink is cold?

Which letter is a vowel?

Z

N E

Which one do you see at night?

Which one means "thank you" in Spanish?

gracias

adiós

Answers

Which drink is cold?

Which letter
is a vowel?

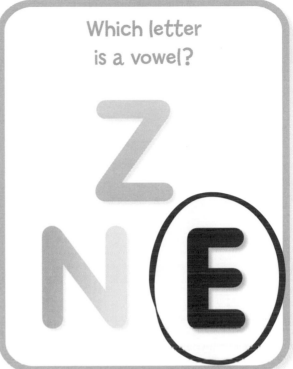

Which one do you
see at night?

Which one means
"thank you" in Spanish?

Questions

Point to the part of the face you use to smell.

Which ball is the big one?

Find all the things that start with the letter **L.**

Point to the part of the face you use to smell.

nose

Which ball is the big one?

Find all the things that start with the letter **L**.

ladder

lamp

lion

lettuce

Questions

How many squares are there?

What is the duck riding?

Which person is a girl?

Which thing starts the same way as "nut"?

How many squares are there?

7

What is the duck riding?

fire truck

Which person is a girl?

Which thing starts the same way as "nut"?

nest

Questions

What is the clown wearing on his head?

Which thing starts the same way as "igloo"?

How many diamonds are there?

Which animal has horns?

What is the clown wearing on his head?

crown

Which thing starts the same way as "igloo"?

ice-cream cone

How many diamonds are there?

3

Which animal has horns?

cow

Questions

Which animal lives here?

Find all the things that start with the letter **S**.

Which animal lives here?

fish

Find all the things that start with the letter **S.**

shark

snowman

saxophone

Saturn

Questions

What's sitting
on the dog?

How many yellow
stars are in the sky?

These letters are all mixed up!
Point to the letters in each
set in the correct order.

What's sitting on the dog?

frog

How many yellow stars are in the sky?

10

These letters are all mixed up! Point to the letters in each set in the correct order.

Questions

What is the correct order for these pictures?

What animal is in the boat?

alligator
goat
cat

Which of these is different?

Answers

What is the correct order for these pictures?

 **2**

 **3**

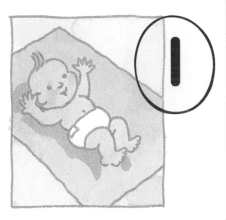 **1**

What animal is in the boat?

alligator

goat

cat

Which of these is different?

Which person is jumping the rope?

Point to the part of the face you use to taste.

What color bead comes next on the necklace?

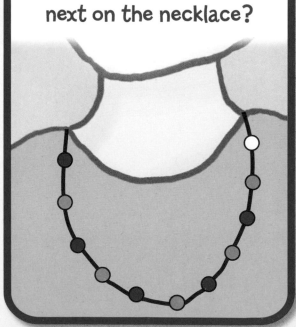

Which one is the farmer?

Which person is jumping the rope?

Point to the part of the face you use to taste.

tongue

What color bead comes next on the necklace?

red

Which one is the farmer?

Questions

What kind of weather do you need an umbrella for?

Which group of coins is equal to the exact price?

What kind of weather do you need an umbrella for?

rain

Which group of coins is equal to the exact price?

4¢

Questions

Point to the easel.

Which of these is exactly the same as the top crayon?

How many vehicles have four wheels?

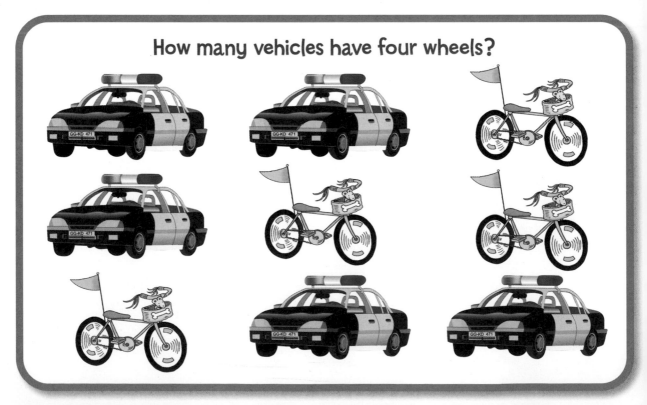

Point to the easel.

Which of these is exactly the same as the top crayon?

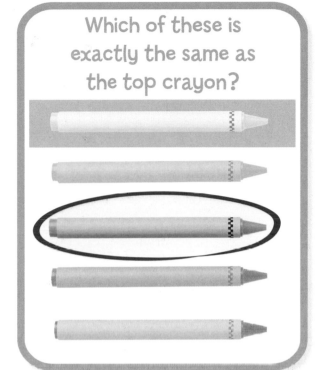

How many vehicles have four wheels?

5

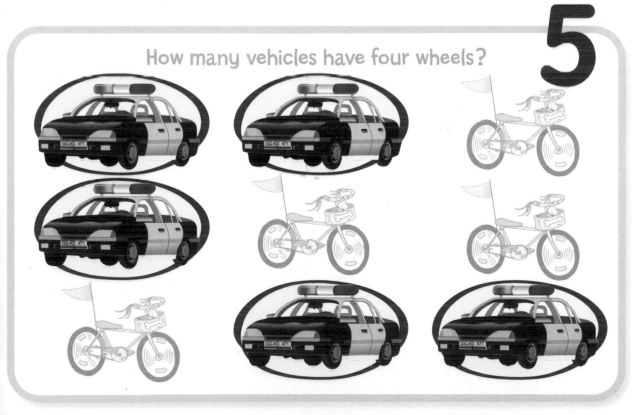

Questions

Which is the oldest?

Which picture matches the word?

frog

Which bowl is the opposite of full?

Answers

Which is the oldest?

Which picture matches the word?

frog

Which bowl is the opposite of full?

empty

Questions

How many candles have stripes?

Which one is Little Miss Muffet?

What do you call a group of people who are all related? Here's a hint: It starts with the letter F.

Which one is floating?

How many candles have stripes?

3

Which one is Little Miss Muffet?

What do you call a group of people who are all related? Here's a hint: It starts with the letter **F**.

family

Which one is floating?

Questions

Find the word "stop" in this picture.

How many of these foods are fruits?

Find the word "stop" in this picture.

How many of these foods are fruits?

3

apple

orange

bananas

Question

How many roller coaster cars are yellow?

How many roller coaster cars are yellow?

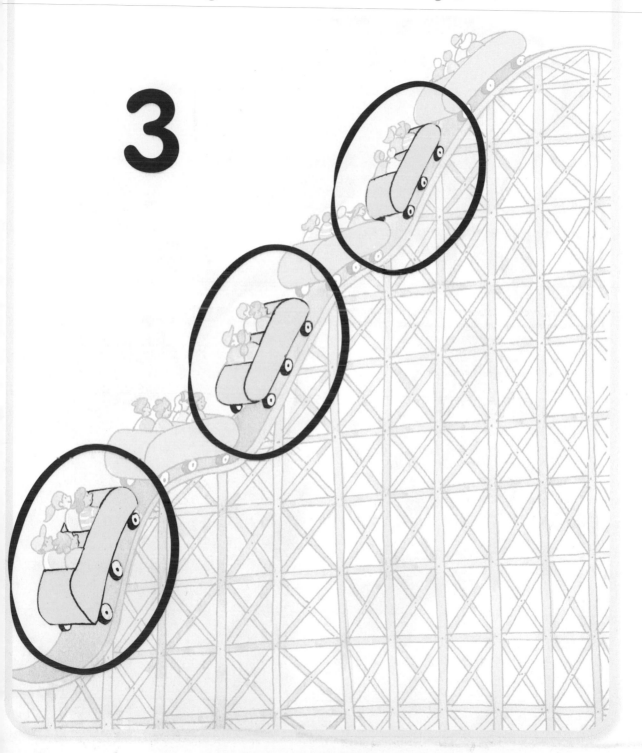

Which letter is a consonant?

U V

E

Are there more orange or pink dinosaurs?

Which person is the mother?

How many dimes are there?

Which letter is a consonant?

Are there more orange or pink dinosaurs?

Which person is the mother?

How many dimes are there?

8

Questions

Are there more ducks or ducklings?

How many apples are red?

Which two things go together?

What do you say when someone gives you a present?

Are there more ducks or **ducklings**?

How many apples are red? **4**

Which two things go together?

pencil

notebooks

What do you say when someone gives you a present?

Thank you.

Questions

What numbers would you dial in an emergency?

Which would you use to dance?

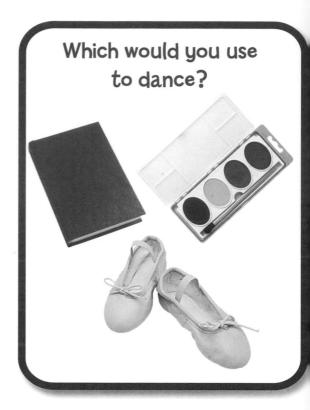

Which animal is upside down?

What numbers would you dial in an emergency?

9-1-1

Which would you use to dance?

ballet slippers

Which animal is upside down?

pig

Questions

Which fruit has two sides that are almost exactly alike?

What is the correct order for these pictures?

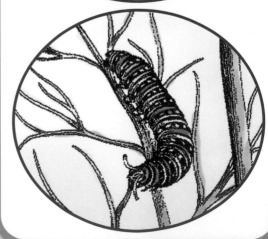

Answers

Which fruit has two sides that are almost exactly alike?

What is the correct order for these pictures?

Questions

Which one means "good night" in Spanish?

 **buenas noches**

estrella

Who sat on a wall and had a great fall?

Which two things go together?

Which one means "good night" in Spanish?

buenas noches

estrella

Who sat on a wall and had a great fall?

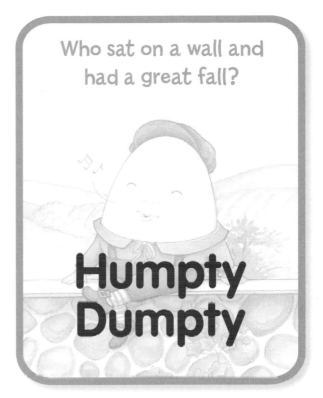

Humpty Dumpty

Which two things go together?

basketball

hoop

Questions

What is the correct order for these pictures?

Which one is on the bottom?

Which person is the son?

Answers

What is the correct order for these pictures?

3

2

1

Which one is on the bottom?

snail

Which person is the son?

Questions

Find the word "go" in the picture.

Point to the bin you'd use to recycle this plastic bottle.

Look out the window. Is the weather rainy, sunny, or snowy?

What do you think the mouse is doing?

Answers

Find the word "go"
in the picture.

Point to the bin you'd
use to recycle this
plastic bottle.

Look out the window.
Is the weather **rainy**,
sunny, or snowy?

What do you think the
mouse is doing?

singing

Questions

How many shirts have polka dots?

Who lives in the igloo?

Who is oldest?

Which children are skipping?

Answers

How many shirts have polka dots?

2

Who lives in the igloo?

Eskimo

Who is oldest?

Which children are skipping?

Questions

What is the correct order for these pictures?

Point to the chopsticks.

Which group of coins is equal to the exact price?

11¢

Answers

What is the correct order for these pictures?

 **2**  **3**  **1**

Point to the chopsticks

Which group of coins is equal to the exact price?

11¢

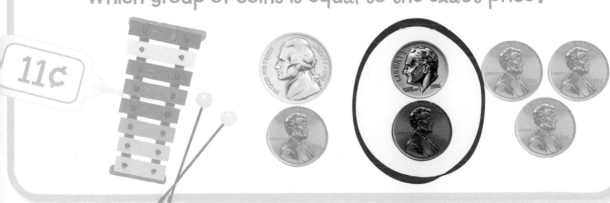

Questions

Point to the mouse.

How many things are hot?

Which two things go together?

What do you wash after using the bathroom?

Answers

Point to the mouse.

How many things are hot?

soup

fire

2

Which two things go together?

dog

bone

What do you wash after using the bathroom?

hands

Questions

Find the word "ice" in this picture.

What do you say when you politely ask for something?

Give me
_____
Please

How many nickels are there?

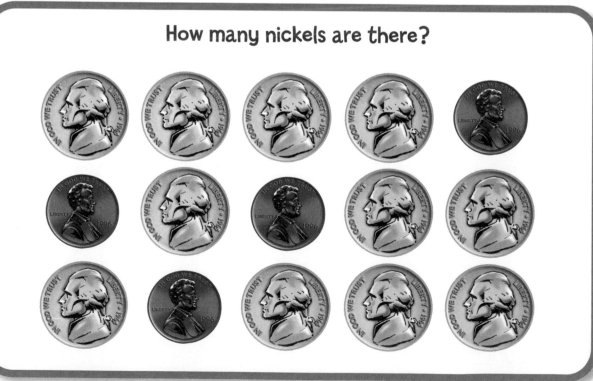

Find the word "ice" in this picture.

ICE CREAM

STRAWBERRY VANILLA CHOCOLATE

What do you say when you politely ask for something?

Give me

Please

How many nickels are there?

Questions

What kind of animal is
hiding on the tree branch?

Find the word "bus"
in this picture.

How many pennies
are there?

What does a
helmet protect?

What kind of animal is hiding on the tree branch?

chameleon

Find the word "bus" in this picture.

How many pennies are there?

What does a helmet protect?

head

CONGRATULATIONS!